To Market, To Market

WRITTEN BY **Anne Miranda**

ILLUSTRATED BY **Janet Stevens**

Harcourt, Inc.

Orlando Austin New York San Diego Toronto London

Text copyright © 1997 by Anne Miranda
Illustrations copyright © 1997 by Janet Stevens

www.HarcourtBooks.com

Library of Congress Cataloging-in-Publication Data
Miranda, Anne.
p.   cm.
Summary: Starting with the nursery rhyme about buying a fat pig at
market, this tale goes on to describe a series of unruly animals that run
amok, evading capture and preventing the narrator from cooking lunch.
ISBN 0-15-200035-6
1. Nursery rhymes. 2. Children's poetry. [I. Nursery rhymes.]
I. Stevens, Janet, ill. II. Title.
PZ7.M657To   1997
95-26326

P   R   T   U   S   Q

Printed in Singapore

The illustrations in this book were done in acrylic, oil pastel,
and colored pencil with photographic and fabric collage elements
on 100% rag Strathmore illustration board.
The display and text type were Elroy.
Color separations by Bright Arts, Ltd., Singapore
Printed and bound by Tien Wah Press, Singapore
Production supervision by Stanley Redfern and Ginger Boyer
Designed by Lydia D'moch

Special thanks to Ideal Market in Boulder, Colorado
—J. S.

To my grandmother, Hattie Evans,
who used to bounce me on her knee
—A. M.

To Coleen Salley, who allowed me to
take her to market, to market;
to Shirley Sternola, for her encouragement;
and, of course, to Dorothy
—J. S.

To market, to market,
to buy a fat PIG.

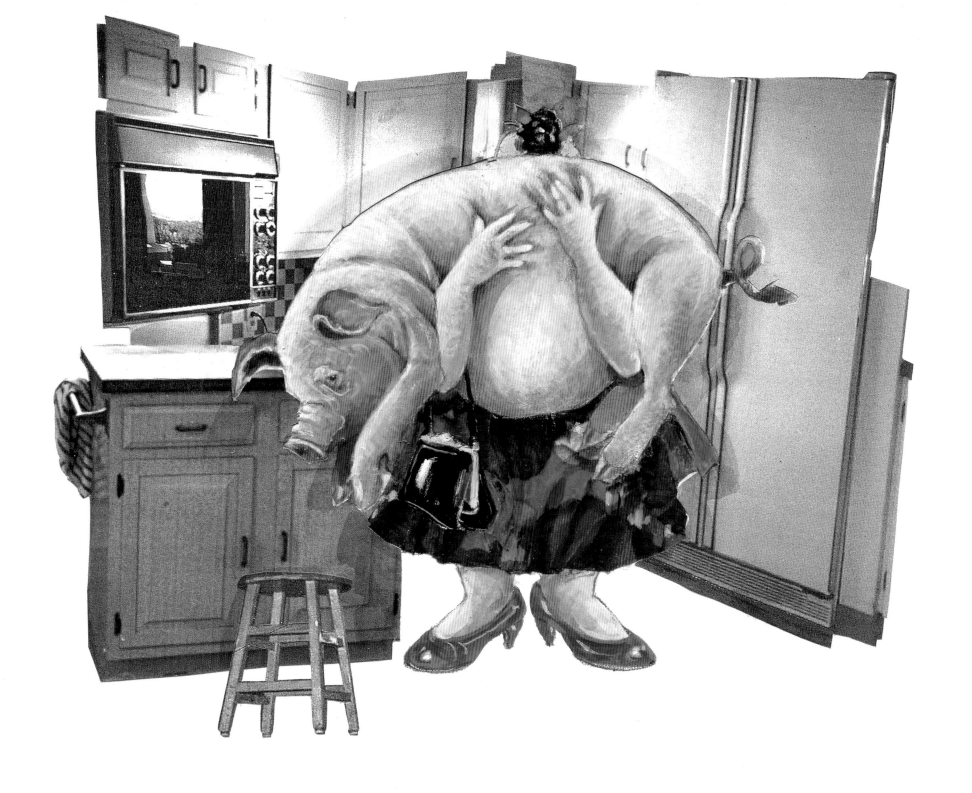

Home again, home again, jiggity jig!

To market, to market,
to buy a red HEN.

Home again . . .

To market, to market,
to buy a plump GOOSE.

Home again . . .

Uh-oh!

The hen's
on the loose.

FROZEN

To market, to market,
to buy a live
TROUT.

Home again . . .

Uh-oh!

The goose
was let out.

To market, to market,
to buy a spring
LAMB.

Home again . . .

Uh-oh! Away the trout swam.

To market, to market, for one milking COW.

Home again . . .

Uh-oh! Where is that lamb now?

To market, to market,
to buy a white
DUCK.

Now the cow disappeared,
and I'm out of luck!

To market, to market,
for one stubborn
GOAT.

The duck
flew the coop,
and the goat
ate my coat!

The **PIG**'s
in the kitchen.

The **LAMB**'s on the bed.

The **COW**'s
on the couch.

There's a **DUCK** on my head!

The **HEN**'s in the cupboard.

The **GOOSE**
is there, too.

The **GOAT**'s
in the closet—
it's chewing
my shoe!

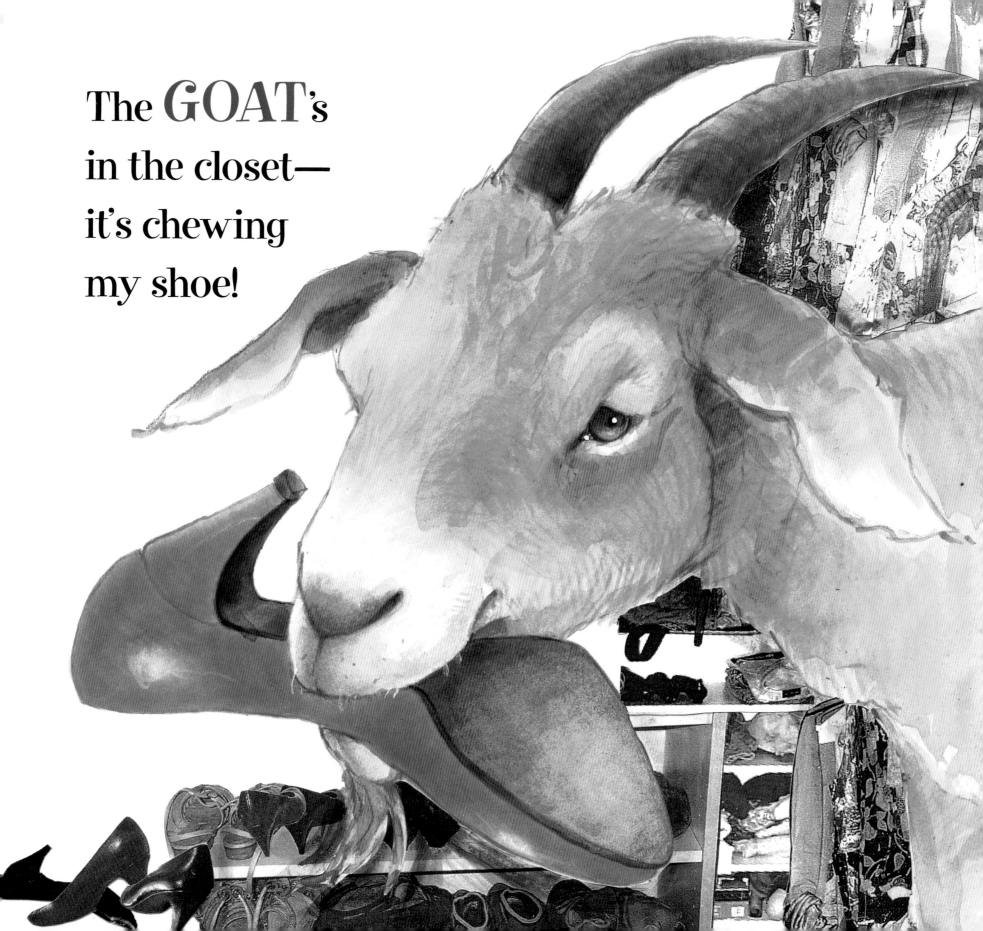

The **TROUT**'s in the bathtub.
This place is a zoo!

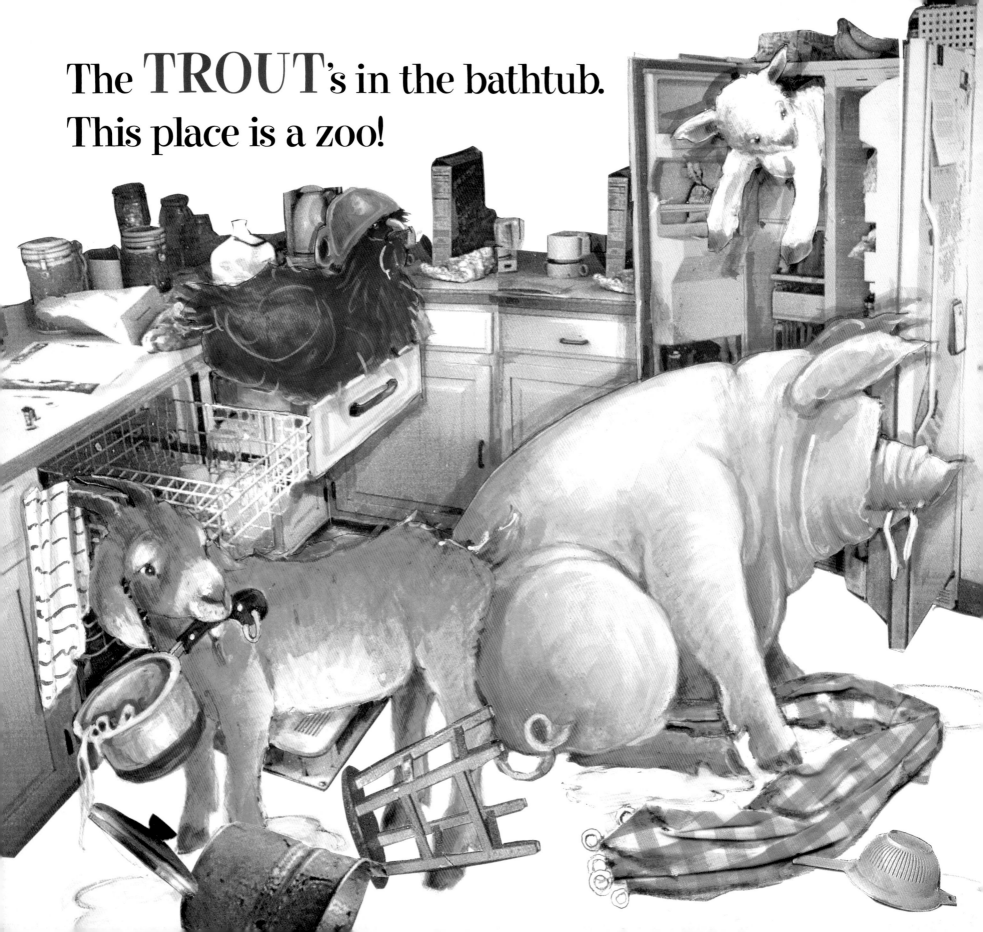

To market, to market,

to buy some POTATOES,
CELERY,
BEETS,

and some ripe red
TOMATOES,

some **PEA PODS** and **PEPPERS,**

and GARLIC and SPICE,

a round head of **CABBAGE,**

a sack of
BROWN RICE.

Add **OKRA**

and **ONIONS**

and one **CARROT** bunch.

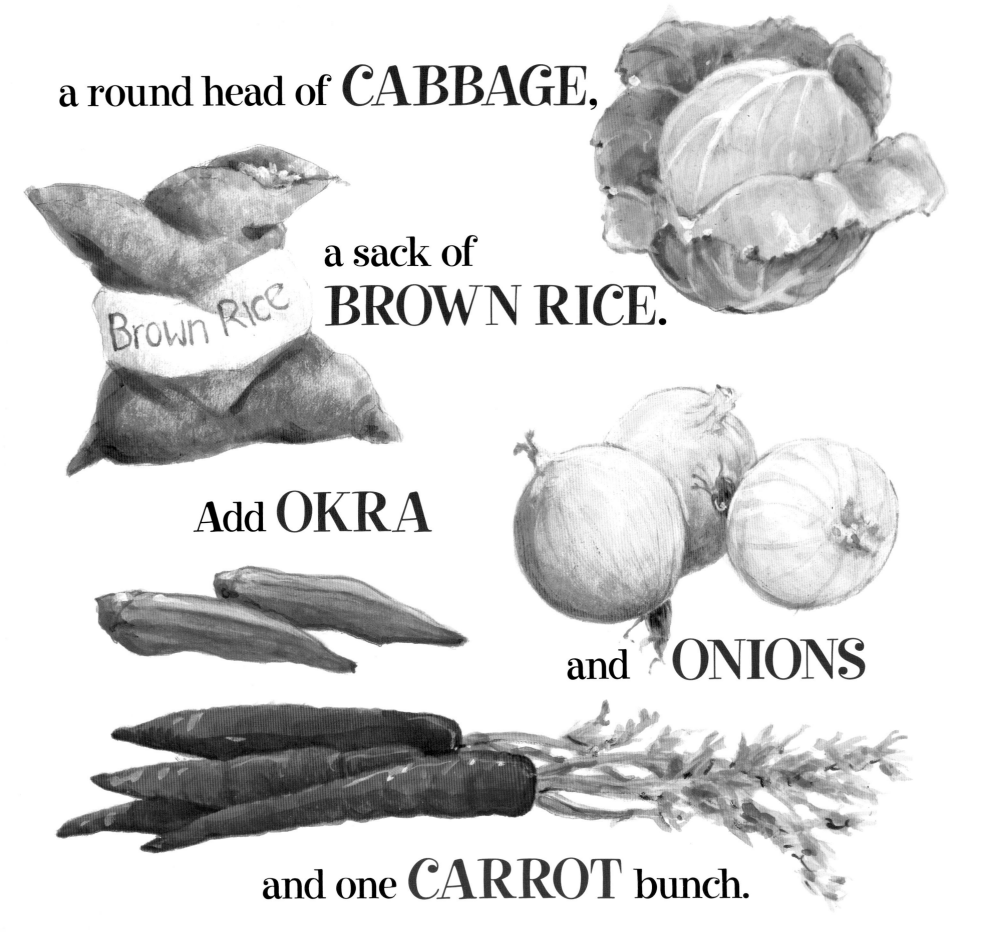

Home again, home again—

hot SOUP

for lunch!